BAD KITTY

Does NOT Like DOGS

NICK BRUEL

SCHOLASTIC INC.

Kitty has been busy.

Now she wants to take a nap.

But not Puppy.

Puppy wants to play.

Puppy wants to play baseball.

Puppy wants to play basketball.

Puppy wants to play soccer.

Puppy wants to play chess . . .

... even though Puppy does not
know how to play chess.

Kitty does not want to play with Puppy.

Kitty does not want to play baseball
or basketball
or soccer
or chess.

Kitty wants to take a nap.

Kitty has an idea.

Kitty wants to play a game called "Sleep."

The player who can sleep the longest wins the game.

On your mark . . .
Get set . . .

SLEEP!

Too bad. Puppy loses the game.

But Kitty wins!
HOORAY!

Kitty does not like dogs.

Special thanks to Rob Steen

No part of this publication may be
reproduced, stored in a retrieval system,
or transmitted in any form or by any means, electronic, mechanical, photocopying, recording, or
otherwise, without written permission of the publisher. For information regarding permission,
write to Square Fish, an imprint of Macmillan, 175 Fifth Avenue, New York, NY 10010.

ISBN 978-0-545-91286-0

12 11 10 9 8 7 6 5 4   17 18 19 20/0

Printed in the U.S.A.   40

First Scholastic printing, September 2015

Book designed by Kristie Radwilowicz

For Richard LaValliere,
who liked dogs very much